THE KNIGHT WITH THE BLAZING BOTTOM

A VERY FIERY FAIRY TALE

SIMON & SCHUSTER

London   New York   Sydney   Toronto   New Delhi

For Katie, Lucy & James

Edited by Polly Whybrow &

Designed by Chloë Bilalis

Simon & Schuster
First published in Great Britain in 2022 by Simon & Schuster UK Ltd
1st Floor, 222 Gray's Inn Road, London, WC1X 8HB
Text & illustration copyright © 2022 Beach
The right of Beach to be identified as the author and illustrator of this
work has been asserted by him in accordance with the Copyright,
Designs and Patents Act, 1988 • All rights reserved,
including the right of reproduction in whole or in part in any form
A CIP catalogue record for this book is available
from the British Library upon request
ISBNs: 978-1-3985-0640-4 (HB) 978-1-4711-9725-3 (PB)
978-1-4711-9726-0 (eB)
Printed in China
1 3 5 7 9 10 8 6 4 2

FSC
www.fsc.org

MIX
Paper from
responsible sources
FSC® C144853

THE KNIGHT WITH THE BLAZING BOTTOM

by BEACH

Our story begins with a knight on the town . . .
Sir Wayne seemed happy, but Dragon was down.

"It's just so unfair,"
he said to his friend,
"Each time I breathe fire . . ."

"...it comes out the wrong end!

Most normal dragons can soar and swoop
But one little fart and I'm looping the loop.

I want to blow flames on knights from afar,
Not blaze through the sky like a shooting star."

"Don't worry," said Wayne, "I've seen so much worse.
You're simply a dragon who's stuck in reverse.
Your frontside is back and your upside is down.
That burn at your stern needs turning around!"

"But how?" said Dragon. "I don't understand."

"Fear not," said Sir Wayne, "for I have a plan!"

"We need to go backwards — and backwards ALL day —
Then back will flip front and your fire's the right way.

It's simply a question of cause and effect.
When forwards is wrong, then back is correct."

"Plan-tastic!" said Dragon, swishing his tail.
"A fix-up this mixed up can't possibly fail!"

So Dragon and Wayne began with their task,
Doing last things first and first things last.

They reversed through the door
THEN used the key,

Un-laid the table

and poured back the tea.

They un-filled the bath
and un-washed their faces,

Un-brushed their teeth in all the wrong places.

They un-dusted, un-cleared, un-put-away mess,
Un-sorted the toys and un-tidied the rest.

And just when it seemed their undoings were done,
They muddled the trouble for double the fun.

Wayne copied Dragon,
he stomped and he roared.

Then Dragon was Wayne
with a swish of his sword.

They mixed and un-matched,
un-stitched without stopping,

Changing, arranging.
Switching and swapping.

They messed as they dressed, putting pants on last.
Then Wayne pulled a face and they laughed and laughed.

"Oh, what a night!" said Dragon with glee.
"The best kind of night there could possibly be!
The two of us make such a marvellous team.
This back-to-front plan has worked like a dream."

"Perfect," said Wayne. "Then it's time to get going.

Fire up those flames
and get ready
for blowing!"

"Now look sharp, stand up straight. Stick out that chest!
Take a deep breath and give it your best."

So Dragon did what a dragon should do,
And he blew
and he blew
and he blew
and he blew.

Nothing.

No smoke or flame of any kind.

No burning in front, no blazing behind.

"Strange," said Dragon. "There should be something alight.
We did all of our wrongs totally right.

Dragon turned slowly and peered at the knight.
"Tell me, Sir Wayne, are you feeling alright?"

"To be honest," said Wayne,
"I don't feel too good.
I feel more Dragon
than a knight really should."

He opened his mouth as if to say more,
But all that came out was a strange little roar.

Then a snort of steam.

Then a smoke-filled growl.

Then an ear-splitting, spark-spitting . . .

"Hot socks!" shouted Dragon. "A fire-filled knight!"
But what happened next was a breathtaking sight.

For warm-hearted Wayne had set light to his suit
With a wonderful, blunderful, thunderful . . .